Napsha
the miracle dragon

Written and Illustrated by

CJ Ryce

Spellbound Publications 1996

*For Michael and Christa
who helped me find
strength and courage and joy.*

Love, Mom

9/99

First Edition

Publisher's Cataloging in Publication

(Prepared by Quality Books, Inc.)

Ryce, C. J.
  Napsha, the miracle dragon / written and illustrated by C. J. Ryce
  p. cm.
  SUMMARY: Napsha, abandoned in a trunk with the other toys, learns about friendship from an unexpected source.
  ISBN 0-9653695-2-8

  1. Friendship-Juvenile fiction. 2. Dragons-Juvenile fiction. 3. Toys-Juvenile fiction.
I. Title

PZ7.R934Na 1996   [Fic]
                                 QBI96-40180

Published by Spellbound Publications
P.O. Box 4778
Rockford, Illinois 61110-4778

Illustrations done in pastel.
Printed and bound by Moore Distributors, Broadview Heights, OH

"Let me out,"
a muffled voice cried,
but only the low moaning
of a distant wind answered.
No one heard the small cry
coming from a run-down trunk,
abandoned in a drafty attic.

"What place is this?"
Napsha muttered as he
pressed against a crack
in the trunk's wall.

"Where am I?"

He stared at the still forms outside the
trunk, but nothing looked familiar. He felt a
hard tug in his chest and sat back on his tail.
Pushing a hand against his seams, he checked
his stitching–his seams were tight. He shook
himself from head to tail–no sawdust fell out.

1

"What's going on?" he cried, "What's happening to . . . me?"

His words trailed off, then stopped. He lifted his head and stared in awe as a picture filled his mind—a picture from a time long ago.

Such a thing is not suppose to happen to a dragon made of cloth, but Napsha didn't know that. All he knew was that Aunt Hilde's beautiful face suddenly appeared before him. The scent of rose water surrounded him as she leaned close and broke a purple thread with her teeth. Then, setting thread and needle aside, she sat back in her chair and looked at him. After a breathless moment, she lifted his chin.

"Hello, my little miracle dragon," she said, and her eyes danced with a smile.

Napsha lost himself in the light of Aunt Hilde's eyes until another picture filled his mind. This time, he saw a four-poster bed and sensed the heat of a crackling fire. When he felt the touch of a child, he gasped.

Napsha knew in an instant where he was. He was where he had been a thousand times before—with Michael.

Michael was wrapped around a post at the foot of his bed staring at the fireplace, lost in dreams. Napsha felt the boy's arm tighten around him and didn't question if what he saw was real or not. He snuggled close to his friend with a sigh.

"Let's read Napsha's story tonight," he heard Aunt Hilde say.

Aunt Hilde sat down next to Michael and spread a worn book across her lap. She turned to the first page, but her voice fell to a whisper as she began to read. Napsha nearly toppled over as the picture in his mind faded then disappeared. He didn't understand—it was only a memory.

3

"No," he said, looking around the darkened trunk in confusion.

"I love you, auntie," he heard Michael say, "you too, Napsha."

Reaching toward the sound, the small dragon cried out, for nothing was there. He stared at streaks of yellow light filtering into the trunk and strained to see Michael's face.

4

"Love," he said, trying to hold on to his friend's words. "Michael said he loved me. What is it? What does it mean?"

He stared at the dark walls surrounding him and felt another painful tug inside his chest. Crossing his arms in front of him, he began to pace back and forth in the corner.

"Love," he exploded at last. "Who cares what it means? What good is it?"

He spun around and charged the wall beating on it until he sank to the floor in defeat.

"Is this it?" he cried. "Is this all that's left for me now?"

Silence closed in around him and he moaned. "I don't care," he said. "If I can't be with Michael, what does it matter?"

Wrapping his tail around himself, Napsha closed his eyes and gave up hope of anyone coming to take him from the trunk. His body began to feel stiff and strangely distant. His thoughts grew hazy, and he let go a sigh. If he couldn't be with his friend, he didn't care about anything anymore . . . but someone did care—about him.

"Please stay," a quiet voice urged. "Your family needs mending."

Napsha raised his head and stared in numb surprise at a brilliant light that shone all around him.

"Mending?" he said shielding his eyes from the intense light. "I had my tail mended once, but I don't know anything about mending. Aunt Hilde did that."

"Where is she?" he blurted. "Where's Michael? Why did they leave me here alone? Michael said he loved me. What did he mean? What is love?"

"What . . . what are you?"

Napsha's mouth fell open when the voice answered him.

"Don't be afraid," the gentle voice said. "Love is with you. It will always be with you. It is how you will mend."

"Me . . . mend, but I'm not torn. What do you mean? Who are you? Where did you come from?"

"Call me Aurael," the voice answered. "As for the rest, you will see."

"See what?" he asked, but the voice and brilliant light were gone. Napsha blinked and looked around as his eyes adjusted to the dim light that once again surrounded him. His gaze fell on an odd collection of toys spread across the trunk.

"See what," he sighed. "There's nothing to see."

The words were barely out of his mouth when, in a blinding flash, Aurael's light brushed past him and beamed across the trunk. Tiny flecks of golden dust shimmered in its soft rays. As the glittering dust fell across the toys, some of them stretched and yawned. Others sneezed and brushed the dust away from their faces.

"Do you see that?" Napsha asked, leaning toward a clown crumpled in a heap not far away. "What is it? Where did it come from?"

"Hmmph!" Blue grunted, as he reluctantly opened one of his painted eyes. "What a dump!"

"No," Napsha said. "I mean that sparkly stuff. Don't you see it?"

The clown shrugged and turned away, and Napsha opened his mouth to speak again, but stared at the clown's back a moment and said nothing. He watched in silence as the shimmering dust settled to the floor and disappeared. When darkness overcame him, he curled up with his head on his tail.

"Love is always with me?" he wondered, yawning and inching closer to the old clown. "Always with me," he repeated softly, and, moving as close as he dared to Blue Clown's hunched form, he closed his eyes.

In the morning Napsha awakened with a start. Nothing stirred in the patched light of the trunk and he shook his head.

"What a strange dream," he said, and glanced at Blue Clown.

Faded and worn, the old clown appeared quite lifeless as he lay slumped against the wall with a round-bellied pup curled up on one of his shoes. The clown was an odd-looking fellow with no hair at all and huge, stitched ears.

As Napsha examined the clown's ear, he felt a strong urge to touch it's soft, worn surface. He reached out, but then quickly pulled his hand back when the ear appeared to twitch.

"Hey, clown!" he yelled. "Can you hear me?"

"Hey! Ho?" Blue grunted, lurching upright. He poked a finger in his ear and turned to glare at Napsha.

"You again," he grumbled. "What in grizzly grease paint are you, anyway?"

"Me?" Napsha asked, staring at the pup at Blue's feet. Pup had rolled off Blue's shoe and now lay on the floor whimpering.

"I . . . I, uh, I'm a dragon. You know—like in the story."

"Dragons!" Blue snorted. "Dragons, pups—all the same to me. Nuisance, I say . . . nuisance."

"No sense," Napsha said, sitting up straight. "What do you mean no sense? Aunt Hilde said talking to me made more sense than talking to most grown ups she knows. She said I was Michael's best friend—a real 'miracle dragon,' just like in the story."

The clown shrugged and slumped back against the wall, but other toys turned to stare.

"Well, that's what she said," Napsha declared. He thrust his chin forward, and a swatch of blue hair fell over his eye.

"A story?" a soft voice asked, and Napsha followed the sound to a pair of emerald green eyes peering at him from beneath thick coils of red hair.

"What story?" Rag Doll asked.

"It's a story about . . . me," Napsha said. "What about it?"

"I like stories, that's all," Rag Doll answered, shrinking away from the dragon's stare.

"You do?"

"Uh huh."

"Even . . . dragon stories?" Napsha asked, his eyes narrowing, and the doll's face lit up. Her curls bounced like wild springs around her head as she nodded, and Napsha's face broke into a grin.

"So do I," he sighed, "but I guess I'll never hear another one, at least, not in here."

Rag Doll lowered her head, and the trunk fell silent until Napsha spoke again, his face flushed with excitement.

"I remember," he said.

"Excuse me," Rag Doll said, turning to look at him.

"I remember the story."

"What story?"

"The story about me, you know, the dragon story . . .

"There once was a time when dragons roamed the earth and wizards were honored for their calling," he said, but then stopped and stared at Rag Doll who had begun to giggle and clap her hands.

"Don't stop," she said. "Go on! Tell me the story. Tell me about the dragons." Napsha thought for a moment and felt a chill of excitement as he remembered.

"Dragon prides lived in a thousand different lands," he said. "Most were known as fierce warriors, but the Grand Dragon of Shakare warned his subjects that wars of fire would destroy them all. He commanded his pride not to fight but to live in a peaceful manner."

"Rubbish!" someone bellowed, and Napsha stopped, startled by the harsh sound. The gloved hand of a tin soldier was raised in a fist.

"Cowards," the soldier declared. "Only cowards run from a fight."

"Oh, Ire, you don't know that," Rag Doll chided, turning her emerald gaze his way. "Besides, he didn't tell them to run away. Listen to the story. Be quiet and listen."

The soldier looked at her a moment then pushed himself to his feet and stomped to the back of the trunk. Napsha watched Ire move back and forth in the shadows, and it took some coaxing from Rag Doll before he spoke again. When the worn pages of his favorite book did at last appear in his mind, he closed his eyes. The first thing he saw was the mighty Grand Dragon.

The Grand Dragon of Shakare was honored and respected by all who knew him. Other Grands came to the land of Shakare to seek his counsel as his pride grew in number and his empire stretched to the foothills of the great mountain. The Grand was pleased by this, of course, but nothing compared to the joy he felt when his son was born. Prince Napsha was born in the month of two moons, a most favorable sign, but the babe was small and quiet and no ring of smoke appeared with his first breath.

"How come I'm so small?" the young prince demanded when he was old enough to follow his mother around. "When will I be as big as pop . . . and when will I be able to fly?"

"Have patience," his mother smiled. "Your time will come. Size is no measure of worth or courage at any rate. Hold truth in your heart and believe in yourself. In time you will understand what matters.

"You don't remember Golith," she said as she blasted twigs from their flat and brushed the ash with her broad tail. "Golith was a sight to behold! The shadow of his wings darkened the entire flatland whenever he circled to land. Still, despite his wondrous size, Golith wasn't able to face his challenge. He ran and hid in the outlands. Your father found him and urged him to come home, but Golith chose to stay in the outlands. He's there to this day, all too often drunk on cantberries."

"What a lizard!" Prince Napsha exclaimed. ". . . Uh, mom, what exactly was his challenge, anyway?"

"The 'challenge,'" his mother said, raising an eyebrow, "is different for each dragon and not so easy to face. In the rite of passage, a dragon must face his deepest fear. One day, you too will have to face your fear. If, on that day, you understand your power, you will know what it means to be Grand. On that day, you will be ready to stand at your father's side."

"I can do that now!" Prince Napsha declared, snarling and jabbing the air with his feet. "I'm not afraid. I'm not afraid of anything."

His mother shook her head and sighed as she watched her son bound across the flat. The prince drew alongside the elders with his head stretched high. Even so, he barely reached his father's knee.

"Twerp," Ire muttered, not missing a beat as he marched back and forth along the back wall of the trunk.

"Who? Who's a twerp?" Napsha demanded, turning to stare at Ire.

"That runt dragon," Ire snorted, "thinks he's so special because his father's some sort of Grand or something. Little twerp, that's what he is."

"Don't listen to Ire," Rag Doll broke in. "Tell me some more about the prince. I like him. He sounds cute."

"Well, I never thought of him as cute," Napsha said, turning toward her with a perplexed look, "but he wasn't a twerp. He was just small and couldn't breathe fire."

"Couldn't breathe fire?" Rag Doll asked.

"No . . . but he was still a prince."

Prince Napsha was born to be a Grand, like his father. When bucks his age began to blow sparks of fire, he could hardly wait to blow fire of his own. He held his breath and let go blast after blast, but all that appeared were tiny puffs of smoke. This was most embarrassing when dragon bucks gathered to play fire hockey. Prince Napsha listened in dark silence as they argued over whose team he should be on.

"You take him!"

"We took him last time. You take him!"

As his friends squabbled, the prince's face grew pinched and grey. No one noticed when he slipped away and ran into the hills. He stopped on a rocky ledge and held his breath till his face turned from purple to blue. He let go a blast, and a thick puff of smoke circled his head. Fanning the smoke away, the young prince coughed and sank to the ground.

"Believe in myself," he choked. "How am I supposed to believe in myself? What good is a dragon with no fire?"

Burying his head in his arms, Prince Napsha cried until his eyes were hot and swollen. He waited until after dark to slip home and spent more and more time alone in the hills after that. As time passed, he came to know nearly every bluff and canyon of Shakare.

The day he came across a flock of ranger birds, he chased them, bounding as high as he could, willing his small wings to fly. He ran for miles whooping and hollering until he tripped and rolled to a stop in the path of a long shadow. Struggling to catch his breath, he looked up. A beast with deep hooded eyes and a strange scent stared down at him.

"Uh, hello," the prince said. "Do I know you? Are you here to see my pop? He's over that way . . . or is it that way?"

Prince Napsha offered a weak smile to the stranger, but three more beasts appeared. The lumbering creatures surrounded the prince and poked at his wings. They didn't speak, just grinned and nodded to each other, and the young prince's stomach twisted in a knot. Jumping to his feet, he bobbed between their legs and ran.

"See, he is a twerp . . ." Ire sneered from the back of the trunk. "Twerp . . . twerp!"

"Twerp . . . twerp?" Fluster screeched, raising her rubbery neck in a flurry of feathers. "Are you making fun of me?"

Fluster flopped about wildly as she tried to stand on her thin, wooden legs. It took a push from the puppet twins before she finally wobbled to her feet. She clattered toward Ire and raised her beak just as his foot shot out in front of her.

With a shriek, Fluster crashed to the floor. Once again the puppet twins rushed to the howling bird's rescue. All three of them moved to a far corner and first one, then another, turned to stare at Ire as a low murmur spread through the toys.

"Please," Rag Doll begged. "Please be quiet. Napsha's telling me a story. Don't you want to hear too?"

The murmuring stopped and several toys gathered around Napsha while he rubbed his forehead and tried to ignore Ire's endless marching.

"What's the matter with him," he muttered, and a swirl of light and color caught his attention.

"Your family needs mending . . . mending," echoed through his head. Napsha's gaze followed the swirl of light until it vanished. Still the words repeated in his head and he listened, wondering what they could mean, until Rag Doll's questioning look brought him back to the story.

"Oh yeah," he said, "The story . . . I was telling you about the beasts in the story. They weren't just big you know."

The beasts surrounding Prince Napsha were huge! They spit balls of fire at his tail, and the frightened prince dodged the stinging balls and ran as fast as he could. He ran without looking back until he reached the great mountain. Only then did he glance behind him, and as he did his foot dropped in a hole. With a squeal, Prince Napsha rolled to the bottom of a foul-smelling pit. Pulling himself up off the ground, he pushed his way to the top of the slippery hole and peered out cautiously.

"Get out of the way! You're blocking the light," someone yelled, and the prince spun around. He lost his footing and rolled to the bottom of the pit once again. This time, he looked up and gasped.

A creature, unlike anything he'd ever seen, stared at him from the hollow of a deep cave. Its face reflected the green of a bubbling beaker at its side, and shadows moved like restless ghosts on the walls around it. The creature held up a knobby stick and pointed in Napsha's direction.

"Out!" he shouted. "Leave now, or by pigs and snakes I swear, a pink-eyed swamp toad you'll be."

The robed being eyed Napsha over thick rounds of glass balanced on his bump of a nose. A wisp of smoke began to wind around the stick in his hand.

Prince Napsha dove behind a rock. He peered out, waiting for a chance to make a run for it. He watched as the curl of smoke moved up the creature's stick then gathered in a puff of smoke around his head.

"Briar bushes!" Napsha exclaimed, stepping out from behind the rock. "Does that happen to you too?"

The being coughed and fanned the smoke from his face. He glared at Napsha, and the young dragon ducked back behind the rock but continued to stare.

The stranger thrust his stick at the smoke that had risen to a cloud above his head, then howled in pain.

"Slimy, stinkin' toad tinder," he cried, quickly lowering his knobby stick, and the hair on Napsha's neck stood on end.

At the creature's shocked words, bright green toads suddenly leaped from the cloud of smoke. They tumbled down around the odd being, disappeared into the folds of his robe, then dropped to the floor. The croaking of the toads echoed through the cave, but the fellow hardly noticed. Gingerly he untangled the hairs of an extraordinarily long mustache that were wrapped around his stick.

Napsha watched in amazement as the toads leaped across the cave, turning over pots and baskets in their path, then vanished one-by-one.

"A wizard!" the young dragon declared popping out from behind the rock. "That's what you are . . . a wizard!"

Slapping his hand across his mouth, Prince Napsha backed toward the cave's entrance. He muttered a quick apology, then scrambled up the steep slope only to roll to the bottom again.

"A wizard?" the creature asked. "I mean, yes, yes, that's what I am . . . a wizard. Yes, yes, indeed, an honorable wizard, of course—Mizrin by name; but what manner of beast dares to appear at my door unbidden?"

He leaned forward, pushing his glasses close to his eyes, then made a strangled choking sound.

"A dragon," he sputtered. "You-you're a dragon!"

Straightening up, he slammed his stick on the floor.

"What do you want?" he demanded. "Why does a dragon seek a wizard? How is it you knew where to find me?"

"It was an accident, sir," Napsha said, rising to face the wizard as he knew a prince should. Wistfully, he glanced at the steep entrance.

"A dragon," the fellow muttered, suddenly unmindful of Napsha's presence. "Odd, most odd. Dragons and wizards are enemies, always and forever . . . enemies. How can this be?"

Mizrin began to pace back and forth, nearly tripping on his long mustache at each turn. He stopped only long enough to ask a question or two. The dragon prince watched him pace and noticed, for the first time, that the wizard was no taller than he.

Mizrin stroked his mustache and paced faster when he learned the young dragon buck could breathe no fire.

"So, this is why you seek a wizard," he said, pressing his glasses to his eyes and examining Prince Napsha closely. "Interesting, most interesting. You may have come to the right place after all.

"Come back tomorrow," he said, dismissing the prince with a wave of his hand. "I believe I have just what you need. It's here somewhere . . . somewhere."

Muttering to himself, Mizrin turned and rummaged through a basket of scrolls. The prince watched a moment then scrambled to the top of the pit and ran home.

Prince Napsha tossed and turned all night unable to think of anything but the wizard's offer. In the morning he watched his friends compete to see who could blow the longest band of fire and knew what he had to do . . .

It was late afternoon when the young dragon found Mizrin's cave again. The ground shook and smoke belched from its dark entrance as he approached. Napsha hesitated only an instant before jumping in. He pushed the stunned wizard to the surface just as flames swept through the cave and licked at his heels.

"Stupid," Mizrin wheezed when he finally stopped coughing. "Clumsy and stupid, that's what I am! I'll never be a wizard—not a real wizard."

"I'm sure that's not true," Prince Napsha said, but the troubled wizard shook his head.

"You wouldn't say that if you knew," he said.

Sinking to a rock, Mizrin turned away from the prince's curious stare. Several moments passed before he let go a deep sigh and explained.

"I was working on a spell to make you think you could breathe fire," Mizrin said, "but the fire wasn't supposed to be real.

"I thought if you believed I could give you such a gift, you would do whatever I asked of you. I was going to say you would have to return to my homeland with me before I could make the fire last. There, I planned to hold you captive and tell my brothers I had taken your fire. It wasn't a very good plan, I know. I just wanted my brothers to honor me for once . . . as a true wizard.

"I think I was supposed to say 'fire back' instead of 'backfire.' Why can't I get it right? Why can't I ever get anything right? Maybe I need new glasses," he said as he removed his blackened spectacles and dabbed at them with his soot-covered robe.

"Go home, dragon," he added in a quiet voice. "I can't help you."

The young prince nodded but didn't move. He stared at the ground lost in thought.

"You must have a good heart, Mizrin," he said after a lengthy silence, "or you wouldn't tell me this, but you would never find honor with such a trick, anyway. It wouldn't be the truth about you and you would know. You'd never be able to believe in yourself. How could any-one else believe in you?

"My mother and father say it's not your size or how well you do something that matters. They say to hold truth in your heart and believe in yourself. When you think about it, how else could you believe in your-self? I guess being honorable is just being the best you can be."

Mizrin turned and stared at Prince Napsha.

"Can it be I have something to learn from one so young, not to men-tion . . . a dragon!" he said and absently rubbed his glasses on his robe as he gazed at the young prince.

Mizrin and Prince Napsha spent many hours together after that eventful day. They pored over scrolls saved from the fire—together. With Napsha's help, the wizard made frogs, lizards and even a white bat appear with the words of his spells, but nothing was ever quite as he expected . . .

The prince left for home later and later each afternoon. He completely lost track of time on the eve of the dark moon. Odd things were said to happen on such a night, and Napsha grew skittish as darkness overtook him on his way home. An owl swooped past him and he jumped and squealed. Laughing nervously, he scolded himself for being such a lizard but then heard heavy footsteps on the path behind him. Noticing an odd scent, he ducked into the shadows.

Staying downwind, Prince Napsha watched as huge beasts passed but a wingspan away. Their scent haunted him.

"It's them," he gasped and slapped his hands over his mouth. He waited until their scent faded, then ran for the wizard's cave.

"Mizrin," he yelled as he tumbled in, "help me! My father and the elders are at ceremony. The dragons—the ones that chased me—I saw them again. My father told me they're sea dragons. They come at night to steal our younglings. Please, come with me! I don't know what to do! They were on the path that leads to my home!"

The two friends raced toward the dragons' flat and nearly collided with the beasts who were already making their way back. The wizard yelled words meant to carry him and the prince away to safety. His words turned to a horrified cry when he crashed to a bumpy stop on a distant mountain ledge—alone.

Mizrin stared blindly at the night sky, his glasses in pieces at his side. Staggering to his feet, he fought back tears. He'd been taught to use formulas and spells, but his magic never worked; he never felt the power the others said was there. Sick of failure, with an aching heart, he raised his staff to the heavens. He would try again, but, this time—no magic.

"Hello," he said hoarsely. "Can you hear me?"

There was no answer, but he cleared his throat and went on.

"My, my . . . friend, the young prince, is in trouble," he stammered. "He is, you know, my friend. I didn't know what a friend was, but he has shown me, and now he needs me. He needs my help . . .

"I don't know what to do!" he cried. "My 'magic' doesn't work. Can you help?"

Mizrin's words trailed off. He shook his head and lowered his staff but then heard the distant squeal of a small friend.

"Please," he begged, his eyes filling with tears. "I can't do this by myself. Is there anything you can do? If you're real . . . If you can hear me, please help him. You can use me. Use me now. Just tell me what to do!"

Ignoring the tears that rolled down his cheeks, Mizrin held his stick high. He closed his eyes and surrendered to the power he'd been told was inside him. An eerie stillness surrounded him as he did, a stillness so deep he could scarcely breathe.

A whisper of air lifted the edge of his robe. It whistled and swirled around him. Faster and faster it whirled until it roared in his ears. The earth trembled beneath his feet and Mizrin struggled to hold his ground, then chills spilled down his back as he felt a power, like thunder, lift and hold him gently—as a child.

"The power," he gasped. "It's real. You're real!

"Thank you," he sobbed. "Oh, thank you."

At that moment, Prince Napsha caught his breath for one more step would send him over the edge of a canyon wall. He searched frantically for any path to safety. Nothing but a sheer drop loomed before him.

"What should I do? What should I do?" he wailed, his heart racing. "Mom says to believe in myself. She says to remember I'm a prince. Ohh . . . I'll be nothing but a footprint if I don't get out of here!"

At that moment his foot slipped. A spray of pebbles plunged into the darkness before him, and Napsha squealed.

"Quit being such a lizard," he scolded, stepping back from the edge. "What's the matter with me? The younglings are in trouble. There's no one to help them—no one but me.

42

Jaw set, Prince Napsha turned to face the beasts behind him. He held his head high and raised his hand as they approached.

"I am Prince Napsha, first-born of the Grand Dragon of the Pride of Shakare," he declared, fighting to hold his voice steady. "I command you! Release our younglings and leave Shakare as you found it . . . in peace."

The huge beasts stopped a moment but then howled with laughter.

"Of course," their leader replied, lowering his head in a mock bow. "We will release them . . . at the ocean's bottom. They will serve us well once we have doused their fire, and you with them, strapling."

The beast reached for him with bared teeth, and Prince Napsha flipped his tail and lunged for a youngling held in another beast's grasp. He threw his head back and yelled as loud as he could for courage. His heart nearly stopped when a deafening roar echoed around him. A brilliant light appeared as well, and the young dragon's fear turned to wonder for he realized the sound and the light were coming from him!

44

Prince Napsha still breathed no fire, but a light, more brilliant than a thousand fires, sliced into the darkness with his breath. It flashed and beamed beyond the mountains, filling the sky until it seemed night had turned to day.

The sea dragons backed away from the young prince, confused and blinded by the light. There was nowhere they could hide, nothing the light's brilliance did not touch. Theirs had been a mission of darkness. It was over.

The beasts dropped the dragon younglings. They turned and fled to their home in the sea with tales of a 'miracle dragon' who could eat the night and devour the cover of darkness . . .

Ire slammed his rifle on the floor, and Napsha jumped and turned toward the sound with wide eyes. Ire had inched up behind the group of toys, listening, and now did an about face. He withdrew to the back wall of the trunk in a huff.

"What a bunch of rubbish!" he jeered over his shoulder. "I suppose you think you're some kind of miracle dragon. 'Miracle dragon,' ha! The only miracle is that your seams are holding together after reaching for a story like that!"

"I didn't make it up," Napsha said, his cheeks pink with embarrassment. "Aunt Hilde read it from a book."

"Stupid . . . stupid story, if you ask me," Ire said and turned and stepped on Pup who was bouncing along beside him. The tiny pup yelped and scampered away.

"Did you see that?" the puppet twins yelled. "Ire stepped on Pup. Let's get him! Get Ire!" Napsha was flipped upside-down and trampled in the stampede that followed. He groped to his feet as other toys piled on top of Ire.

"Thanks a lot!" he blustered, then squealed and rolled over on his back. He lay there staring at his foot. It was flat! It had been flattened in the stampede. He shook it furiously, then pulled himself to his feet and hopped about muttering to himself.

"Trouble," he snapped at Ire. "Why are you always causing so much trouble?"

Shaking more sawdust into his toes, Napsha limped to a far corner. He lay there in silence, but half-forgotten words stirred in his mind.

"Your family needs mending," he heard, " . . . mending," and light and color swirled around him.

"Aurael," he said staring at the light, "Aurael, is that you?" Deep ridges formed on his brow as Aurael's gentle words echoed in his mind for he didn't understand.

"Stop!" he cried. "Stop saying that. I can't mend anything. Why do you keep saying that?"

Napsha covered his ears until Aurael's voice was quiet. He had no idea how much time passed before he rejoined his friends, but time has little meaning to a cloth dragon anyway.

One by one Napsha befriended the other toys in the trunk. The memory of his time with Michael began to fade as days passed, then weeks, then months. It was, in fact, a bright, cool afternoon years later when Napsha awakened from a restless nap filled with dreams and haunting memories. Napsha shook his head wondering if he was still dreaming when he heard a familiar sound. Grunting and groaning, he pushed himself to the top of Jack-in-the-box.

"Children," he shouted as he peered through the trunk's keyhole. "I see children! One, two . . . maybe more," he announced as he twisted and turned, trying to see.

"Get out of the way! You're blocking the light!" a harsh voice bellowed, and Napsha jumped. His foot slipped off Jack's box, and he crashed to the floor, face down.

"You can choose now, Napsha," a voice whispered. "You can choose to mend."

Shaking the words away, Napsha tried to stand, but his legs gave way beneath him and he sank to the floor. When he looked up, he saw Ire staring at him.

"It was you," Napsha cried. "You yelled at me. What's your problem anyway? There are children out there. Don't you care?"

Pulling himself to his feet he scowled at the soldier, and Ire turned and marched away.

"Didn't you hear me?" the angry dragon yelled. "I said there are children out there! They'll play with us . . . like Michael did."

"Rubbish!" Ire exploded. "Michael left you here because you were old and ugly and he didn't like you anymore. Those kids won't want to play with you either. You think you're better than me, but you're not! You're old and ugly and you're never going to get out of here . . . not ever!"

A sharp pain shot through Napsha's chest, and he tightened his fists.

"Don't say that," he cried. "That's not true! Michael loved me. He said he loved me."

Flipping his tail, Napsha stomped toward Ire, ready to fight, but the scraping of a key in the trunk's lock stopped him.

"What's the matter with him?" he blustered. "Why is Ire so different? Why does he have to be so mean?"

Napsha caught his breath when a familiar voice answered him.

"Ire's not so different," Aurael's quiet voice said, "like the wizard, not so different at all."

"The wizard?" Napsha asked. "You mean Mizrin, the wizard in the storybook? Ire's not like Mizrin! Mizrin was just lonely and thought nobody cared about him. He and Prince Napsha were friends. They vowed to be friends forever, even after the wizard left to go home. Ire's not like the wizard. He's mean!"

"Ire doesn't know about love yet," Aurael said softly. "He doesn't know that love is inside him. He's angry and confused because he thinks he's old and ugly and no one wants to play with him. You could help him see things in a different way."

Napsha was quiet for a moment then frowned.

"What about me," he exclaimed. "You said love was inside me. How could love be inside Ire too?"

"There's love in everyone," Aurael answered. "You don't like some things Ire has done, but that's not what Ire is. Take a closer look. Look at him now. The past is gone," and then Aurael's soft voice was gone as well. Napsha blinked and looked around, his anger suddenly replaced with questions. He looked at Ire, closely, and realized he'd never done that before unless there was trouble.

51

"Ire, lonely?" he wondered. "I don't think so," but he moved toward the tin soldier trying to see his face.

"What?" Ire demanded when he turned and saw Napsha beside him. "What's the matter now?"

"Nothing, I . . . I mean, your face. I saw something. How do you turn on one foot like that, anyway? You're pretty good at that."

"Good?" Ire asked, and stopped and stared at Napsha with wide eyes.

"Yeah . . . That's it," Napsha said. "That's the look! That's the look I saw on your face before—when I fell. I've never seen that before."

Ire's cheeks turned crimson. His mouth opened, then closed.

"You were worried about me, weren't you?" Napsha said, examining him through narrowed eyes.

"I don't worry about anything," the red-faced soldier said and moved away, but Napsha followed him.

"I've seen you watching us play sometimes," Napsha said. "Don't you ever get lonely, Ire?"

Ire's steps slowed.

"Maybe you're right," Napsha said, running his hand across his forehead. "Maybe we won't ever get to play with kids again, but we can still play with each other. Maybe you could even teach me to march. I know I'd never be as good as you, but—what do you say? It might be fun."

Ire stopped and turned.

"Fun?" he asked.

"Yeah, fun. What do you say?"

"Fun," Ire said again and pushed the bill of his helmet back and scratched his head.

Napsha suddenly felt like giving Ire a hug. To Ire's embarrassment, he did, and a hush fell across the toys. The trunk's heavy lid began to creak and groan. Napsha looked up and watched as a sliver of light moved down the trunk wall. It spilled across the floor, and the small dragon's head began to spin.

"Your family needs mending," he said under his breath, "mending . . ."

He recalled the time he'd been mended—when the heart at the end of his tail had torn away. It fell on the floor, and he remembered how lonely it looked laying there—separate and alone.

Napsha's gaze swept across the faces of the toys he'd come to know so well since he'd been left in the trunk. One face had always stood apart from the rest—separate and alone.

"Ire," he said. "Ire . . . torn?"

"That's it, isn't it?" he exclaimed, his eyes lighting up. "We're a family— all of us here, together—like a family!"

"If I make friends with Ire, is that what Aurael means by mending my family?" he wondered.

Turning toward Ire, Napsha searched his face in wonder. Ire smiled a small, shy smile, and Napsha grinned. He threw back his head in triumph for he was certain he was right and he finally understood! He knew the meaning of those words—the words that had haunted him for so long.

No sound was heard as the small dragon threw back his head to roar, but an explosion of light appeared above him. Rainbows of cascading color glittered in the bright sunlight, and the dragon's mind turned to the story of "Napsha, The Miracle Dragon." He recalled the magnificent light that had appeared with Prince Napsha's deafening roar.

"Miracle dragon," he wondered, "me?"

Then, another memory flashed through his head. He recalled the first time a soft voice had comforted him and brought him a message of Love and the promise of friendship.

"Aurael," he said. "Aurael, is that you?"

"Love will always be with you," a quiet voice answered, and one last burst of color swirled around the happy, cloth dragon as gentle hands lifted him from the trunk.

Books Available From:

Spellbound Publications
P.O. Box 4778
Rockford, Illinois 61110-4778
(815) 397-1218